Paddington at the Beach
Text copyright © 2008 by Michael Bond
Illustrations copyright © 2008 by R. W. Alley
For information address HarperCollins Children's Books, a division of HarperCollins
Publishers, 10 East 53rd Street, New York, NY 10022.
www.harpercollinschildrens.com

Library of Congress catalog card number:
ISBN 978-0-06-168767-9

09 10 11 12 13 SCP 10 9 8 7 6 5 4 3 2

First American edition, 2009
Originally published in Great Britain by HarperCollins Children's Books as
Paddington Rules the Waves in 2008

Paddington
at the Beach

MICHAEL BOND

Illustrated by **R. W. ALLEY**

HARPER

An Imprint of HarperCollinsPublishers

Nothing much goes on at the seaside
that seagulls don't know about.
So when Paddington went down
to the beach early one morning,
he soon had company.

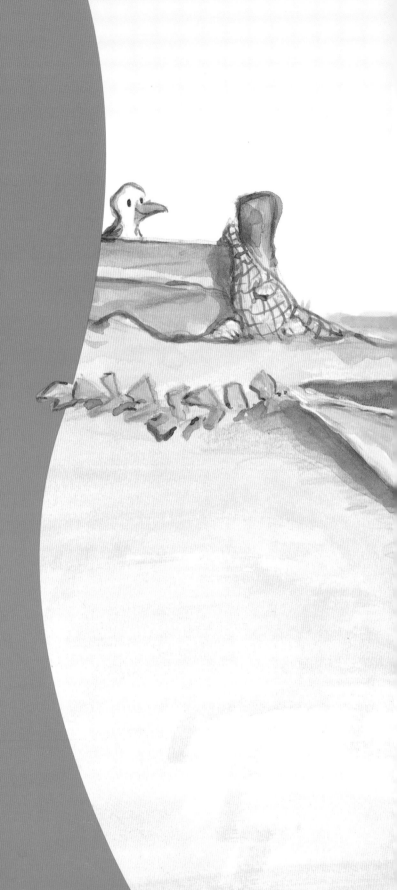

"It's a bear,"
cried seagull number 1,
"and he's digging
up *our* beach!"

"He's made a sand castle,"

said seagull number 2.

"Look how pleased he is."

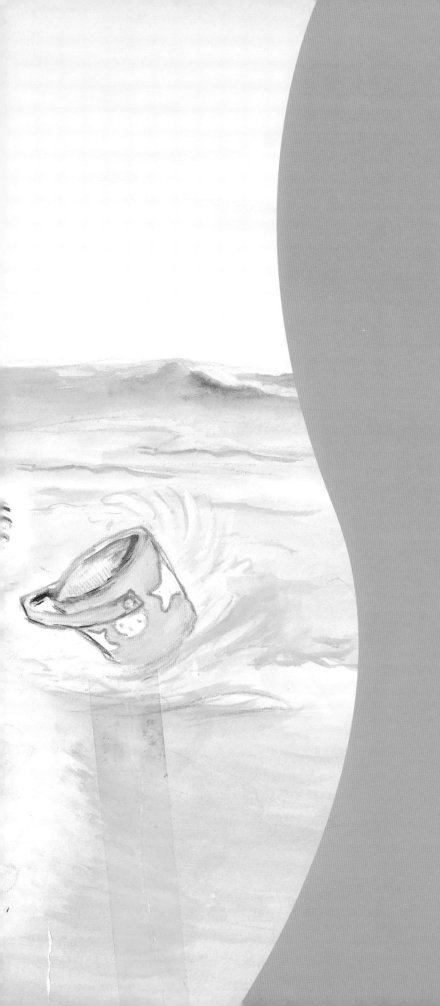

"Now he's lost his bucket,"
said seagull number 3.
"I could have told him
that would happen.
Screech! Screech!"

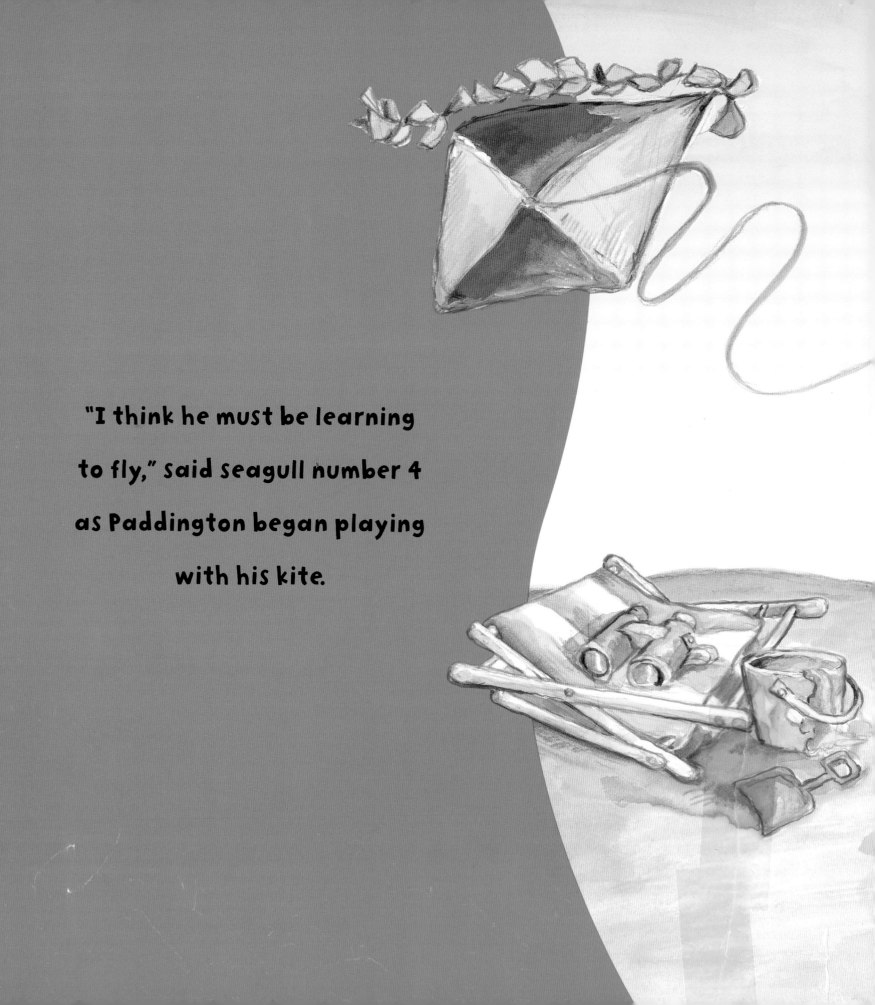

"I think he must be learning to fly," said seagull number 4 as Paddington began playing with his kite.

"He's much too heavy for that,"

screeched seagull number 5.

"What did I tell you?"
it cried, as seagull number 6
joined them.

As Paddington was looking

out to sea for his kite,

seagull number 7 flew in.

"Look!" it cried.

"He's got a bun in his pocket!"

While Paddington
struggled with his deck chair,
seagull number 8 landed.
"I'm hungry," it screeched.
"Shall I try giving the bun a peck
and see what happens?"

"Wait until there are more of us,"

hissed seagull number 9.

Sure enough, a moment later,

seagull number 10 arrived.

"Here goes!" called one at the back.

And they all made a dive.

"Seagulls don't know everything,"
said Paddington when they had gone.
"I always keep a marmalade sandwich
under my hat, just in case!"